CARTWHEELS

CW00871710

Mrs Simkin and the Very Big Mushroom

Linda Allen

Illustrated by

Margaret Chamberlain

Hamish Hamilton
London

First published in Great Britain 1986
by Hamish Hamilton Children's Books
Garden House 57–59 Long Acre London WC2E 9JZ
Text copyright © 1986 by Linda Allen
Illustrations copyright © 1986 by Margaret Chamberlain

British Library Cataloguing in Publication Data
Allen, Linda
Mrs Simkin and the very big mushroom.——Cartwheels
I. Title II. Chamberlain, Margaret III. Series
823'.914[J] PZ7

ISBN 0–241–11730–5

Colour separations by Anglia Reproductions
Typeset by Katerprint Co. Ltd, Oxford
Printed in Great Britain by
Blantyre Printing and Binding Ltd
London and Glasgow

One morning Mrs Simkin said,

"Stanley, there is a very big mushroom in the garden."

"I will cook it for our breakfast," said Mr Simkin.

Mrs Simkin laughed. "I think you had better look at it first," she said.

"It is *enormous*!" Mr Simkin cried.
"I told you so," said Mrs Simkin.
"You couldn't eat all that mushroom if you chewed and chewed all day long."

"I could break a little bit off," said Mr Simkin.

"No, don't do that, Stanley," Mrs Simkin said. "It would be such a pity to spoil it."

"Well, what shall we do with it, then?" asked Mr Simkin.

Mrs Simkin looked up at the sky. It was clear and bright.

"It is going to be a very hot day," she said. "We could use the mushroom as a sunshade."

"What a good idea!" cried Mr Simkin. "Let's have our breakfast in the garden."

Mr Simkin made the tea and toast. Mrs Simkin laid the table.

They sat in the shade of the very big mushroom, eating their breakfast.

The lady next door looked over the hedge.

"What are you doing?" she asked.

"We are eating our breakfast under our mushroom," said Mrs Simkin. "Would you like to join us?"

The lady next door shook her head.

"I don't think so," she said. "It doesn't look very safe."

When they had finished breakfast, Mr Simkin said,

"What are you going to do today, dear?"

"I'm going to tidy up the larder in the kitchen," said Mrs Simkin. "What are you going to do, Stanley?"

"I am going to make a bird-table," said Mr Simkin.

"Oh, you don't have to make one, Stanley," said Mrs Simkin. "We could use the mushroom as a bird-table."

"What a good idea!" cried Mr Simkin. "I'll fetch the ladder."

Mrs Simkin tidied up the larder. She found a stale loaf of bread, a piece of old smelly cheese and some chocolate pudding.

"The little birds are going to have a feast!" she said.

Mr Simkin climbed up the ladder and put the food on top of the mushroom.

And all the birds came down. They began to peck at the loaf of bread and the piece of cheese.

When the birds tasted the chocolate pudding they became so excited that their cries could be heard far away.

Birds came flying in from all around. They caused such a fuss that all the people in the street came to see what was going on.

"What a lot of birds!" they cried.

They went home to fetch their cameras and began to take pictures of the birds.

Nobody saw the dark clouds in the sky. Nobody heard the thunder, until it was too late.

The rain came down hard and fast.

"Come into the garden!" cried Mrs Simkin. "Come and shelter under our mushroom."

So all the people in the street ran to shelter under the mushroom.

It was so big that nobody got wet.

When the rain stopped, they all went home.

"What an interesting day it has been," said Mrs Simkin, as she went upstairs to bed.

“It was your good ideas that made it so,” said Mr Simkin proudly. “I hope you have some more good ideas tomorrow.”

But when they looked out of the window the next morning, they saw the mushroom lying on its side.

It had fallen over during the night.

"What a pity!" sighed Mr Simkin.

"I told you it didn't look safe," said the lady next door. "*Now* what are you going to do with it?" she asked.

"I shall make it into mushroom soup," said Mrs Simkin.

"What a good idea!" cried Mr Simkin.

They had to make the mushroom soup in a dustbin in the garden. The smell from the soup was delicious.

All the people in the street came to see where the delicious smell was coming from.

Mrs Simkin gave everyone a bowl of hot mushroom soup. They all said it was the best soup they had ever tasted.

When the people had finished eating, they all had a dance in Mrs Simkin's garden.

Even the lady next door joined in.

"What an interesting day it has been," Mrs Simkin said, as she went upstairs to bed.

"Yes, most interesting," agreed Mr Simkin. "I wonder if we will find another big mushroom growing in the garden tomorrow?" he said.

And do you know what?
They did.